One Dark Night

Lisa Wheeler
Illustrated by Ivan Bates

GULLANE
CHILDREN'S BOOKS

Published in Great Britain in 2003 by

CHILDREN'S BOOKS

Winchester House,
259-269 Old Marylebone Road, London NW1 5XJ
First published in the USA in 2003 by Harcourt, Inc.

1 3 5 7 9 10 8 6 4 2

Text copyright © 2003 by Lisa Wheeler
Illustrations copyright © 2003 by Ivan Bates
Published by arrangement with Harcourt, Inc.

The right of Lisa Wheeler and Ivan Bates to be identified as the author and illustrator
of this work has been asserted by them in accordance with the Copyright, Designs
and Patents Act, 1988.

A CIP record for this title is available from the British Library.

ISBN 1-86233-534-6

Manufactured in China

In memory of my good friend Linda Smith,
the bravest mouse I ever knew
—L. W.

For George, with love
—I. B.

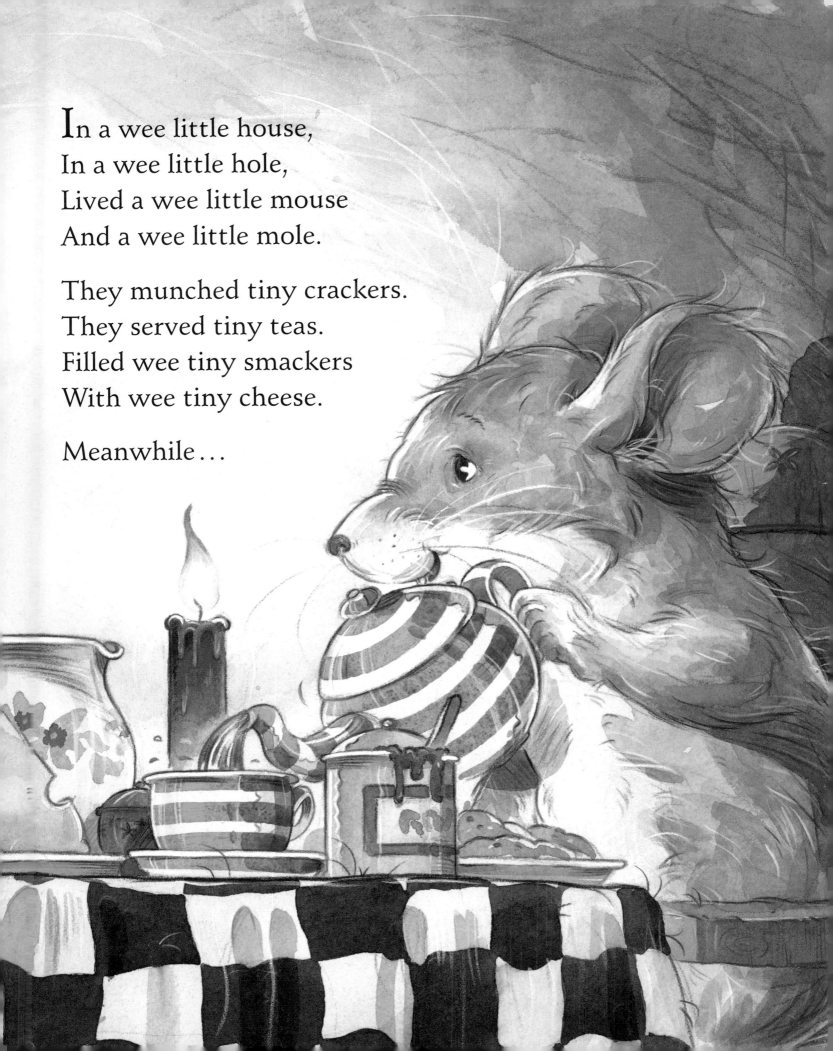

In a wee little house,
In a wee little hole,
Lived a wee little mouse
And a wee little mole.

They munched tiny crackers.
They served tiny teas.
Filled wee tiny smackers
With wee tiny cheese.

Meanwhile…

In a BIG GIANT lair,
Near a BIG GIANT glen,
Lived a BIG GIANT bear
In his BIG GIANT den.

He growled BEASTY growls.
He stomped BEASTY feet.
He stuffed BEASTY jowls
With a BIG BEASTY treat.

Then, one dark night . . .

The two teensy friends
Left their wee tiny house.
"I'm scared of the dark,"
Mole whispered to Mouse.

"There's no need to fear,"
Mouse said with a sigh.
Then the moon disappeared
Behind clouds in the sky.

Meanwhile . . .

In the BIG GIANT lair,
Near the BIG GIANT glen,
The BIG GIANT bear
Stomped around in his den.

He peered out the door.

He tramped and he paced.

He craved
something fresh
With a rich,
meaty taste.

Meanwhile...

With a SQUISH-SQUASH-A-SQUISH
And a TROMP-TRIP-A-TROMP,
Mouse and Mole trudged
Through the mush-mucky swamp…

Under sharp thistle thorns,
Into marsh-misty wood,

To the BIG GIANT glen
Where a gnarled oak stood.

Meanwhile...

The bear licked his chops,
Heard his BIG tummy groan.
"I'M HUNGRY!" he roared.
But he waited. Alone.

"We're lost!" shouted Mole.
"Don't fret," the mouse said.
"I'll climb up this tree
And spy what's ahead."

From tree trunk to branch,
Mouse pushed to the top.

Fragile twigs snapped.
But Mouse didn't stop.

"What do you see?"
The teensy mole cried.
"It looks like a cave—
With a light on inside!"

From deep in that cave
Came a BIG GIANT growl.
"I want something to eat
And I want it NOW!"

Bear threw open the door,
Stomped out of the den,
Bared BIG sharp white teeth,
And charged into the glen.

Mouse perked his ears.
Heard SNARL-SNUFF-A-SNUFF.
"SOMEthing is coming!
And that SOMETHING sounds tough!"

Mole shivered. Mouse shook.
Their fur stood up straight.

The SOMETHING was Bear,
Who grumbled …

"YOU'RE LATE!"

Then they skipped hand in hand,
From the glen to the lair,
For a BIG GIANT feast

With their best friend BIG Bear.